Popular Elizabethan Tunes

for Recorder and Guitar

Selected and Arranged by
Frederick Noad

Ariel Publications
New York · London · Tokyo · Sydney · Cologne

e d c b a
© Ariel Publications, 1977
A Division of Music Sales Corporation
All Rights Reserved

All arrangements © Copyright 1977 by DORSEY BROTHERS MUSIC LIMITED
78 Newman Street, London W1P 3LA
No extracts from this book may be used without the permission of the publishers.

International Standard Book Number: 0-8256-9963-0

Distributed throughout the world by Music Sales Corporation:

33 West 60th Street, New York 10023
78 Newman Street, London W1P 3LA
4-26-22 Jingumae, Shibuya-ku, Tokyo 150
27 Clarendon Street, Artarmon, Sydney NSW 2064
Kölner Strasse 199, D-5000, Cologne 90

Contents

Introduction

The pieces selected for this book were amongst the best known at the end of the reign of Elizabeth I, and continued in popularity well into the 17th Century and later in some cases. Evidence of their universality is afforded by the many settings by composers of the time, and in the case of the Dowland tunes by their printing in both song and instrumental form and their constant recurrence in hand-written books.

Both recorder and guitar were popular in Elizabethan times, though the guitar would commonly have had only four strings (paired for extra resonance). There is no recorded example of the two instruments being used together, but the loose nature of consorts of the period makes such a combination possible.

The arrangements have been made with particular regard to the wide separation between soprano recorder and the modern guitar. Thus the guitar parts tend to be high, and the recorder parts in the lower part of the available register to achieve a satisfactory balance. This had the additional advantage of making some of the tunes available to the alto recorder as well as the soprano.

Some transposition has been necessary to adjust to the best keys for each instrument. However as far as possible the original structure of the contemporary accompaniments has been preserved in the guitar parts.

If a little practise is needed for the players to master these arrangements, I believe that the final effect will be found to be much more satisfying than that achieved with the more usual oversimplified versions.

The Carman's Whistle

TRADITIONAL
(William Byrd)

Robin Is To The Greenwood Gone

TRADITIONAL
(Thomas Robinson)

Recorder

Guitar

Hartes Ease

Anthony Holborne

Heigh Ho Holiday

Anthony Holborne

Tarleton's Resurrection

John Dowland

11

The Night Watch

Anthony Holborne

13

As I Went To Walsingham

TRADITIONAL

Greensleeves

TRADITIONAL
(Francis Cutting)

Recorder

Guitar

Captain Digorie Piper's Galliard

John Dowland

La Rossignol

ANONYMOUS

20

The Right Honourable Robert
Earl Of Essex, His Galliard

John Dowland

My Lord Willoughby's Welcome Home

TRADITIONAL
(John Dowland)